THE
GADGET WAR

BY BETSY DUFFEY

Illustrated by Janet Wilson

A TRUMPET CLUB SPECIAL EDITION

For Charles, the real gadget wiz

Published by The Trumpet Club, Inc.,
a subsidiary of Bantam Doubleday Dell Publishing Group, Inc.,
1540 Broadway, New York, New York 10036.
"A Trumpet Club Special Edition" with the portrayal of a trumpet
and two circles is a registered trademark of Bantam Doubleday Dell
Publishing Group, Inc.

ISBN 0-440-83034-6

This edition published by arrangement with Viking Penguin,
a division of Penguin Books USA Inc.

Set in Plantin
Printed in the United States of America
December 1994
1 3 5 7 9 10 8 6 4 2
OPM

CONTENTS

SOMETHING'S UP

Something was up!

Ms. Haycock walked into her third grade classroom holding a pile of green construction paper. Kelly Sparks looked up with interest. Construction paper meant a project and to Kelly, projects meant inventing.

She reached into her desk and took out a small toolbox. Her desk was different from any other desk at Danville School.

The other desks were filled with pencil boxes, packs of crayons, and notebooks. Kelly's desk was filled with gadgets. Wonderful gadgets.

There was a gadget to send notes and a

gadget to get notes. There was a gadget to dust the erasers and a gadget to hold Kelly's books open to just the right page. There was even a gadget to make the recess bell ring early!

Kelly Sparks was an inventor. By the latest count she had made 43 inventions—gadgets, she called them. And she was only in the third grade.

Ms. Haycock began to pass out the pieces of construction paper. "Today is the first day of Career Week," she said. "On these slips of paper, answer the question, 'What do you want to be when you grow up?' Then draw a picture to go with it."

"Bo-ring," a voice whispered from the back of the room.

Every year now for three years their teachers had asked them to answer the same question. Kelly's eyes sparkled. To her the assignment was not boring at all.

Ms. Haycock had covered the bulletin board beside the door with a picture of the city. "It takes all different kinds of careers to make the city run," she said. "When you finish, come up to the board and put your paper on the correct building."

The room was quiet as the twenty-three third graders bent over their pictures. One by one, twenty-two kids came up and put their pictures on the board—nine policemen, five astronauts, and eight ballerinas.

Ms. Haycock frowned. It didn't seem to be what she had in mind. You can't run a city with nine policemen, five astronauts, and eight ballerinas.

Kelly still worked at her desk. The kids watched Kelly as she finished her project. They watched her as she headed up to the bulletin board.

Kelly liked the expectant looks that the other kids gave her. She liked to be the one to try something different.

She liked it when Ms. Haycock said (in a very nice way), "You never know what's going to happen with Kelly around!"

Kelly lifted up her paper and stuck it right in the middle of the board. It didn't lie flat like the other papers. It bounced and bobbed out from the bulletin board.

Ms. Haycock looked up over the top of her glasses.

"Cool!" someone called out.

It was on a spring. On the paper was a face—not drawn with crayons or markers like the other kids used, but made out of metal things—screws, nuts, bolts, and washers.

Two washers made the eyes. A bolt for the nose. A small piece of rubber tubing for the mouth. All over the top of the head were glued curly shavings of wood that looked a lot like Kelly's curly brown hair.

Beside the face, Kelly had written two words—two special words that could only describe Kelly Sparks:

GADGET WIZ!

The kids clapped and cheered. They loved Kelly's gadgets.

With her gadgets Kelly could solve any problem. Even Ms. Haycock would come to Kelly if she had a problem that needed fixing. Most inventions started with a problem. Kelly loved to read about inventions.

A candy maker had a problem. During the summer months his chocolate candy melted before he could get it to the store. He needed a harder candy. Bingo! Life Savers were invented.

Whitcomb L. Judson had a problem. He was overweight and couldn't bend over far enough to lace his boots. He needed an easy way to fasten them. Bingo! The zipper was invented.

All through history people had problems, and all through history people had been making inventions to solve their problems. It had always seemed so simple to Kelly.

She smiled at the class and took a bow. As she bowed and the kids cheered, Kelly was completely happy and completely unaware that the biggest problem she had faced yet in her life was about to walk through Ms. Haycock's door.

The problem's name was Albert Einstein Jones.

HATE AT FIRST SIGHT

Tap. Tap. Tap.

The laughter and cheers stopped short when the kids saw a familiar shadow through the frosted glass door of the room.

Hardeman!

The principal was at the door. Mr. Hardeman was a strict principal. He never smiled and always walked with his hands clasped behind his back.

Everyone sat quietly in their seats. Nobody wanted to get in trouble with Hardeman!

Tap. Tap. Tap.

Mr. Hardeman tapped on the glass again.

Kelly still stood at the bulletin board beside the door. She opened it.

It was Hardeman, but he was not alone. Beside him was a boy in a blue baseball cap. The cap said YANKEES on it. He had on jeans and a T-shirt.

It was the T-shirt that caught Kelly's attention. In big blue letters it said YOUNG INVENTOR'S CAMP.

Kelly felt a twinge of jealousy. Young Inventor's Camp! A minute ago she had never even known that there was such a thing and now she had the feeling that she had missed out on something wonderful.

"Ms. Haycock, this is Albert Jones," Mr. Hardeman said. "Albert Einstein Jones. He will be in this class for the rest of the year."

EINSTEIN! Kelly felt another twinge of jealousy. Why couldn't *her* mother have named *her* something wonderful like *Einstein?* Her middle name was Frances. Some people had all the luck!

The boy was looking at the bulletin board where Kelly's sign was still bobbing up and down. He looked back at Kelly, then back at the sign one more time.

He frowned at the sign. Then he frowned at Kelly.

He seemed to know right away that the sign was Kelly's and for some reason that Kelly couldn't understand he didn't seem to like it.

Their eyes met. They did not smile at each other. Instead, he reached up to his cap and twisted a button on the side of it.

The top of the cap flipped down and a rubber tongue stuck out at Kelly.

There was muffled laughter from the class.

As fast as the tongue popped out it was gone. Ms. Haycock and Mr. Hardeman were still chatting. They hadn't seen a thing.

Kelly looked at the boy. Her eyes narrowed. She knew the difference between laughing *with* someone and laughing *at* someone. The kids were laughing *at* Kelly and it was this boy's fault. Without a word she walked back to her seat.

She had heard of "love at first sight." It happened all the time in the old movies that

her mom liked to watch on TV. In the movies, "love at first sight" happens like this:

A man and a woman are sitting across the room from each other. Their eyes meet. They fall in love instantly.

It was a little like that with Kelly and Albert—except when their eyes met you would have to call it "HATE at first sight."

Albert was given a desk across the room from Kelly.

Mr. Hardeman left. The class relaxed.

Kelly did not relax. She had a bad feeling about Albert. She watched as Ms. Haycock passed a green slip of paper to him.

She saw him take another hard look at her Gadget Wiz paper on the board. Then he began work on his own paper.

He looked up at her once with a sly kind of smile. Kelly looked down at her desk quickly.

The bell rang. The class lined up to go home. As he walked out, Albert stuck his paper on the board. He had folded his paper so that you couldn't see what it said. On the end of the paper was a string. *Pull,* he had written beside the string.

One by one, as the kids passed through the door to go home, they each pulled the string. Kelly was at the end of the line.

As each kid pulled the string, two small paper doors popped open. When they saw what was underneath, each one looked back at Kelly. Some of them giggled.

Kelly had that "being laughed at" feeling again. She had the feeling that somehow the words on Albert's paper had something to do with her.

I don't care what it says, thought Kelly. *I don't care a bit. I'm not even going to look!* But when it was her turn to pull the string, she decided to do it.

She pulled the string and the two little doors on the green paper flipped apart. Her mouth dropped open.

There were four words on the page underneath. Four words that stung like a slap in the face. She looked up at her paper.

GADGET WIZ!

She had been so proud of it.

When she looked back at Albert's paper her pride was gone. On his paper, under the doors, he had written:

THE *REAL* GADGET WIZ!

INVENT IT!!!

One person can make a lot of difference in the world. Kelly could just look in her *Inventor's Guidebook* to see that.

Life wouldn't be quite so good without the one person who invented cookies, or pencils, or even toilet paper.

Life might be better without the one person who invented bombs, commercials, or even homework.

It only took one person to invent the elevator. One person to invent sneakers. One person to invent Coke.

And now it seemed that it took only one

person to change Kelly's life from perfect to perfectly horrible. Albert Einstein Jones was that one person.

When Kelly got home she went straight to her room. Her room usually made her feel special. No one had a room like Kelly's. It was an inventor's room.

Where other kids might have had boxes of Barbie dolls or model airplanes, Kelly had boxes piled high with all the things that she might need for her inventions: gears, wheels, wire.

Where other kids might have had piles of games or coloring books, Kelly had piles of invention plans.

And, on the walls, where other kids might have had posters of rock stars, Kelly had large pieces of pegboard covered with screwdrivers, wrenches, clamps—every kind of tool.

Today Kelly's room did not make her feel special. The one extra-special thing about Kelly had been her gadgets. The other kids liked her gadgets. She was sure they liked *her* because of her gadgets. She had always been the only one who could invent things. Like a thief, Albert Einstein Jones had taken away her specialness.

If I'm not the only Gadget Wiz, then I am a nothing, she thought. *A big nothing!*

A tear rolled down her cheek as she remembered that afternoon. It fell down on the *Inventor's Guidebook* in her lap.

It was Albert's fault! He was the problem. Suddenly she wasn't SAD anymore. Suddenly she was MAD. But what could she do about it? She opened her *Inventor's Guidebook*. On the first page were the three steps to inventing.

IDENTIFY THE PROBLEM.
IDENTIFY WHAT YOU NEED TO
    SOLVE THE PROBLEM.
INVENT IT!!!

It seemed so easy until *you* had a problem.
   She looked again.

IDENTIFY THE PROBLEM.

That part was easy. Albert Einstein Jones was the problem.

IDENTIFY WHAT YOU NEED
TO SOLVE THE PROBLEM.

She chewed on the tip of her hair for a minute while she thought: A gadget to make Albert Einstein Jones disappear. That was impossible. Kelly sat staring at the page for a full five minutes without moving.

Finally, it came to her. She would make a gadget that would show Albert Einstein Jones who the *real* Gadget Wiz was. A gadget that might not make him disappear but that would make him think twice before he bothered Kelly Sparks again.

Something was up!

She turned to the Inventor's Log section of her *Inventor's Guidebook*. At the top of a page it said GADGET #44. In her fattest, brightest red marker she wrote three words:

FOOD-FIGHT CATAPULT.

She closed her book with a bang, jumped down from her bed, and in a voice almost like a battle cry she yelled:

It didn't take much time to make it—only five minutes.

It didn't take much material to make it—only a coat hanger.

It didn't take any tools at all to make it—only her two hands.

But, even though it was made without taking time, material, or tools, Gadget #44, the food-fight catapult, was one of Kelly's greatest inventions.

She sat at her desk admiring it. To someone else, Gadget #44 might seem like only a bent piece of wire with loops at each end.

Many inventions in the world didn't seem like much until you understood them. Look at a paper clip, cork, or eraser. If you just thought of them as a piece of metal, a piece of bark, and a piece of tree sap, that's all they would ever be.

It takes an inventor to see the paper clip in a piece of metal, the cork in a piece of tree bark, the eraser in a piece of tree sap. Or in

Kelly's case, the food-fight catapult in the coat hanger!

It was all a matter of seeing the potential in things. POTENTIAL was Kelly's favorite word. It means possibility. Kelly prided herself on being able to see the potential in things. She knew it was important. All inventors had to be able to see potential.

What if Chester Greenwood had not seen the potential of a piece of baling wire and two pieces of beaver fur? Earmuffs would never have been invented.

If some college students at Yale had not seen the potential of a pie pan from Frisbie's Pies, the Frisbee would never have been invented.

Worst of all, if Ruth Wakefield had not seen the potential in a block of Nestlé Semi-Sweet Chocolate, chocolate chips would never have been invented!

If Kelly Sparks had not seen the potential of an ordinary coat hanger, Gadget #44 would never have been invented!

Yes, it was the perfect invention. Not exactly right for the fall science fair. But, it was useful anyway. You never knew when you might need a food catapult at Danville School. Especially with Albert Einstein Jones around.

Kelly picked up the catapult and headed downstairs to the kitchen. The inventing was over for now, time for the testing to begin.

WHOOPS!!

Kelly opened her notebook and laid it out on the kitchen counter. She liked to keep a close record of all her testing. Under the words *Food-Fight Catapult* she wrote *Testing*.

She poked her pencil behind her ear and rubbed her hands together expectantly. Testing was the best part of inventing.

She would have to hurry. She didn't have much time before her mom came home from work and she had the feeling that her mom would not approve of testing a food-fight catapult in her kitchen.

Her mom had not been pleased the time

Kelly tested her Automatic Frog Catcher in the bathtub. How could Kelly have known her mom was about to take a bath?

She had not been pleased the time Kelly had tested her Automatic Bed Maker on her bed. Was it Kelly's fault that the timer had gone off too early? Too bad her mom was still in the bed.

Her mom just didn't understand her inventions and she probably would not understand this one, either.

She would have to finish testing before her mom got home. She needed something to use for the test. For a food-fight catapult she needed food, of course. She tried the cupboard.

Half a box of Crispy Cocoa Crunches. Too small.

A bag of cheese puffs. Too light.

A jar of marinated artichoke hearts. Too disgusting.

Next she tried the refrigerator.

Shriveled lettuce. Too limp.

A quart of milk. Impossible.

A carton of eggs. Too messy . . . but . . .

Kelly opened the cardboard egg carton care-

23

fully and looked at the eggs. There were ten eggs in the carton. Kelly looked at the catapult on the counter, then back at the eggs.

Should she or shouldn't she? Her mother would kill her if she made a mess. But . . .

Kelly could just imagine the eggs flying through the air. They would land right in the bowl. No mess at all!

Kelly smiled at the thought of it. The eggs would be perfect. At the top of the page under *Food-Fight Catapult—Testing,* she made two columns:

Test Food   *Results*

Under the *Test Food* column she would write down each food tested. Under the *Results* column she would write what happened.

She wrote down the first test food:

GRADE-A MEDIUM EGG #1

She would write in the results after the test.

Kelly positioned the bowl on the other side of the kitchen. She put the egg on the wire loop and pulled it back and forth a few times to get a feel for it. It felt just right.

She pointed it at the bowl. She pulled the loop back.

Ready . . . aim . . . FIRE!!!

The egg sailed across the kitchen magnificently. Kelly's mouth dropped open at the sight of the flying egg. It was headed right toward the bowl . . . almost.

Splat! The egg splatted on the wall to the right of the bowl.

Kelly looked at the wall. Drippy blobs of egg dripped down her mother's wallpaper. Pieces of shell clung to the wall and floor.

But . . . the catapult had worked! The egg flew!

Gadget #44 was a success!

No real damage done, she thought. *The wall is washable. The floor is washable, too.* She would clean it up later. Right now she had some adjustments to make on her invention.

Gadget #44 had real potential!

Under the results column she wrote:

WHOOPS!!

Then she smiled and got out another egg for testing.

GADGET GROUNDED

GRADE-A MEDIUM EGG #2

Kelly picked up another egg, loaded it into the catapult, and pulled the wire loop back.
Ready . . . aim . . . FIRE!!!
Splat!!
A little closer to the bowl, but this time too far left. Too bad about Mom's philodendron.
Well, she decided, a little egg might be good for a plant anyway, like fertilizer. She almost had it!
WHOOPS! she wrote again.
Kelly looked at the carton. There were eight

eggs left. She had only planned to use two but neither one had hit the bowl. She just knew that if she tried one more egg, she could do it.

GRADE-A MEDIUM EGG #3

She made a slight adjustment on the catapult, picked up another egg, and pulled back. Ready . . . aim . . . FIRE!!!
Splat!!
Too bad about the overhead light. It had needed cleaning anyway. She would clean it later. Her mother would thank her.
WHOOPS! she wrote again.
Now she was determined to hit the bowl.

GRADE-A MEDIUM EGG #4

Ready . . . aim . . . FIRE!!
Meowwwwww!!!!!
Whoops! The cat!
ANIMAL INTERFERENCE, she wrote under the results column. The cat left the kitchen leaving a trail of eggy paw prints.
Kelly looked down at the carton. There were six eggs left. She just had to get one in the

bowl. She began to hurry.

GRADE-A MEDIUM EGG #5

Quickly she loaded another egg and pulled back.

The egg flipped back out of the catapult. Before Kelly could duck, it landed right on the top of her head. Cold, wet egg-white dripped down her hair. The yolk slid down her forehead and dropped onto the floor in front of her.

BACKFIRE! she wrote.

She didn't even stop to clean it off. Scientists have to deal with discomfort. She was too determined to stop.

She got out another egg.

GRADE-A MEDIUM EGG #6

Ready . . . aim . . . FIRE!!!
Whoops! The microwave.

GRADE-A MEDIUM EGG #7

Whoops! The spice rack.

GRADE-A MEDIUM EGG #8

Whoops! The toaster.

GRADE-A MEDIUM EGG #9

Whoops! The coffee maker.

Kelly began to think that she would never get it right. The food-fight catapult was of no use if it could not hit a target.

She looked down at the egg carton. There was only one egg left. She only had one more chance.

She looked hard at the bowl. For a moment, in place of the bowl she imagined a face—ALBERT EINSTEIN JONES.

With new energy she took the next egg out of the carton. She never looked away from the bowl. She never stopped imagining the face.

"Creep!" she said to the bowl.

She put the egg on the loop and slowly pulled back.

She squinted her eyes at the bowl.

Ready . . .

aim . . .

FIRE!!!!

Grade-A Medium Egg #10 flew across the

kitchen with perfect aim. Kelly held her breath.

Splat!! The egg hit.

Kelly stared at the bowl in disbelief! The egg had landed directly in the center of the bowl.

Direct hit!!!!

She did it! The food-fight catapult was a success!

Kelly jumped up and down, twirling her food-fight catapult over her head. *"I did it!"* she yelled. *"I did it!"*

As she jumped, her foot hit a puddle of egg white and down she went onto the kitchen floor.

She didn't care. In her excitement she didn't notice the puddle of egg that she was sitting in.

She didn't notice the egg still dripping from her hair.

She didn't notice the eggs on the wall, the plant, the toaster, the light, the window, or the spice rack.

And she didn't notice the sound of her mother's key turning in the lock of the kitchen door.

Whoops! Testing over!

"KELLY FRANCES SPARKS!!!!"

Her mother stood in the doorway, her hands on her hips. For the first time, Kelly looked around the kitchen. Eggs were everywhere. Sticky blobs of egg white were stuck to the wallpaper. Bits of shell covered the floor. Yellow egg-yolk puddles dotted the floor and counter. When she had been shooting the eggs, it didn't seem like so many. It looked like a lot more than ten eggs now.

"It was an experiment, Mom," Kelly started. "I was testing . . ."

"Kelly!" her mother interrupted, "you are officially grounded, GADGET GROUNDED! No more experiments! No more inventions! And *no* more gadgets in this house!"

She took the catapult out of Kelly's hand and threw it into the trash can. "And in fifteen minutes, I expect this kitchen to be spotless!"

Her mother hurried up the stairs, stepping hard on each step. Kelly watched the top of the trash can swing back and forth. She blinked back the tears. There was nothing sadder to

Kelly than the sight of one of her precious gadgets in the trash.

No more gadgets! Gadget grounding was the worst possible punishment to Kelly. Especially now, when she had a problem and needed her gadgets the most.

Her mom's words still rang in her ears. "Gadget grounded!" Then she remembered her mom's *exact* words, "No more experiments! No more inventions! And no more gadgets in this house!"

In this house!

This gadget was not needed *"in this house!"* This gadget was needed at Danville School. Quietly she opened the trash-can lid and took out Gadget #44.

Today, testing was over. Tomorrow it would be needed for real combat.

GOTCHA!!

The next morning Kelly loaded up her backpack for school. She put in her homework, her books, a comb, a pack of gum. . . . She paused.

She pulled the food-fight catapult out of its hiding place in the top of her closet and looked at it.

Should she or shouldn't she? It had already caused her a lot of trouble.

Well, just because she took it to school didn't mean that she had to use it. She put it in the backpack.

She started to zip up the backpack, but

paused again and looked around the room. There might be some other things here that could come in handy. Just in case you-know-who wanted to start something again today. Pretty soon the backpack was bulging and Kelly was on her way.

BRRINNNGGGG!!!

The last bell was ringing just as Kelly hurried into the classroom. She saw Albert watching her as she sat down. He had a mean grin on his face.

As soon as she sat down she knew that something was wrong.

Oooooooooooooooooo gross!

Something was wet on Kelly's seat! Something wet and squishy had been on her seat when she sat down. She felt the back of her jeans. Gross! Now the back of her jeans was wet and squishy, too.

How could it have happened? She felt again. There was something like a flat sponge on her chair. Like a flat WET sponge.

She looked over at Albert. He was grinning.

She could tell immediately that he had done it. He licked the tip of his finger and made an imaginary mark in the air as if he were keeping score and had just scored a point. Without making a sound his lips formed the word, *Gotcha!*

Kelly pulled out the wet sponge-thing and dropped it under her desk. She was so mad that tears stung in her eyes. She would not cry.

She wanted to raise her hand and tell Ms. Haycock, but she didn't. None of the kids in her class had noticed and she didn't want them to know about her wet pants. How embarrassing.

It would be better just to sit quietly and wait for them to dry. She remembered back in kindergarten when Tucker Johnson used to wet his pants in class. He would almost make it to the recess bell when a big puddle would begin to form under his desk. Kelly could remember the big wet spot on the back of Tucker's pants and how the other kids had laughed at him. She didn't want to be laughed at again today.

She had to make sure no one saw her pants.

She sat back and prayed that she wouldn't have to go to the front of the room.

Please, she prayed, *don't let me get called to the board!*

Please, don't let me break my pencil lead and have to go up to the pencil sharpener.

Please, don't let me get picked to pass out papers today.

Please . . .

"Kelly! . . . Kelly Sparks!" Her prayers had not been answered. Ms. Haycock was calling her.

"Yes, Ms. Haycock."

"Kelly, I said, 'Would you lead us in the Pledge of Allegiance?' We are waiting!"

THE PLEDGE OF ALLEGIANCE!!!

How could she go up in front of the class and lead the pledge? Not only would she have to stand in front of the class but she would have to turn around and face the flag! Her wet bottom would be facing the class.

"Uh, Ms. Haycock." How do you say no to your teacher?

"Kelly," Ms. Haycock was frowning. She

liked to get the class started on time. *"We are waiting!"*

Her jeans were cold and clammy and stuck to the backs of her legs. The spot on the back of her jeans was darker than the rest of her pants. She could hear a few giggles as she walked slowly up to the front of the room.

No one knew about Albert's trick. They probably all thought that she had wet her pants! The giggles increased when she turned around to face the flag.

Kelly's face was on fire with embarrassment. With her eyes on the floor, she began.

"I pledge allegiance to the flag . . ."

From the back of the room she could hear Albert's voice, louder than all the others saying the pledge.

". . .with liberty and justice for all."

Albert Einstein Jones, she thought as she finished, *you will not get away with this. You will get your justice!*

She did not look up when she finished the Pledge of Allegiance.

She did not look up as she walked back to

her desk. She did not even look up after she sat down at her desk. She felt like she could never look up again.

All through the morning, through reading and math and social studies, she stayed at her desk and thought of only one thing—REVENGE!

THE *REAL* GADGET WIZ

When it was break time, Kelly did not get up or move from her seat. There was still a big wet spot on the back of her jeans. She was too embarrassed to get up again.

All the other kids went out into the hall to the water fountain or to the bathrooms. Albert left with them.

Kelly made her move. Quickly she slipped over to Albert's desk. She opened it.

Wow! She had never seen anything like it. It was full of gadgets. There was a list on top of the gadgets. At the top of the list it said:

WAR GADGETS
by THE *REAL* GADGET WIZ.

Kelly quickly read the list of war gadgets.

1. Pants Wetter
2. Spitball Cannon
3. Smell Gel
4. Sticky Chalk

The first gadget, Pants Wetter, had a big check beside it. Of course: it had already been used!

There were a lot of gadgets on the list. Life at Danville School was getting dangerous.

She closed the desk, but before she went back to her seat she left a little surprise for *him*. In place of his pencils she put two of her own special gadget pencils—pencils that did not write.

"Class, sit down for your spelling test," Ms. Haycock said.

Perfect! thought Kelly.

Across the room she watched Albert get ready for the spelling test. He got out a piece of paper and lined up his pencils at the top of his desk.

Kelly smiled. They were not *his* pencils. He was in for a big surprise.

"The first word is . . . *disaster* . . . *disas-*

ter . . ." Ms. Haycock always said the words twice. Then she would not repeat them. No questions were allowed during the test.

Kelly wished that she had taken time to study the night before. She had been too busy cleaning the kitchen.

Desaster, she wrote on her paper beside number 1. Then she erased it and wrote *Dizaster*. That looked right.

She looked over at Albert. He was desperately trying to make the pencil work. He was writing over and over, pressing the pencil down harder and harder.

Disaster was the perfect word for Albert's spelling test.

Kelly grinned.

Albert stopped trying to write and looked hard at the pencil.

"The next word is *impossible* . . . *impossible* . . ." Ms. Haycock said.

Kelly grinned again. Another perfect word!

Albert picked up the next pencil and tried to write with it. He stopped writing and looked at his paper. His face was red. A little trickle of sweat dripped down the side of his face. He raised his hand and waved it in the air.

"Now, Albert," said Ms. Haycock, "we have a rule about questions during a spelling tests—no questions allowed. Just do your best. The next word is . . ."

Kelly didn't hear the next word. She looked over and realized that Albert was staring directly at her.

She looked back at him. She licked her finger, lifted it into the air, and gave herself an imaginary point. *Gotcha*, her lips said.

Albert's mouth fell open. He picked up both pencils and looked at them closely. He looked back at Kelly. He hit the desk with his fist. Then he put the pencils down and put his head down on his desk. He had given up on the spelling test.

It didn't feel as good as Kelly thought it would. In fact, she felt bad for Albert. He was going to fail his first spelling test at Danville School.

She looked back at her paper and began to think about how she could get a pencil to Albert. Should she try to pass one to him? Should she apologize?

Just as she was beginning to feel like helping Albert, something wet and disgusting hit her on the side of the face. She suddenly remembered what the next gadget was on Albert's list—*Spitball Cannon*.

A big, wet blob of spitball fell down from her face onto her spelling test. Now she didn't feel one bit bad. Now she felt *mad*. When the spelling test was over, instead of apologizing she started her own list of War Gadgets.

At the top of the list she put FAKE PENCIL and put a big check beside it. Of course: it had already been used! Then she smiled a sly kind of smile as she went on to finish the list.

THE GADGET WAR HAD BEGUN!!!

THE *REAL REAL* GADGET WIZ

Kelly's list was quickly finished. She read it over proudly.

WAR GADGETS
by
THE *REAL REAL* GADGET WIZ

1. Fake Pencil
2. Spy Snooper
3. Lipstick Smear Gun
4. Stink Ball
5. Double Gum Shooter
6. Food-Fight Catapult

She saw Albert watching her—*spying* on her! *I'll show him*, she thought.

She held up her list of War Gadgets. Albert was far enough away that he could see that it was a list of War Gadgets, but he could not read what was on the list.

He squinted his eyes trying to read the list. He clenched his fists.

Good, she thought, *he's mad*.

Albert grabbed his list out of his desk.

He borrowed a pencil and began writing furiously on the paper. Then he held it up for Kelly to see.

Kelly couldn't see exactly what it said but she could see that it was twice as long as it was before.

Albert must have added about six War Gadgets to his list.

Kelly couldn't stand to be outdone.

She started adding more weapons to her own list. She could make them later with the supplies in her backpack.

7. Potato Gun
8. Pencil Breaker
9. Slime Slinger

She held up her list again. Albert looked at the list. His face got a little redder. He began to write again. Pretty soon Kelly was writing down more War Gadgets, too. The lists went on and on.

Kelly stopped writing and looked down at her list. It covered two pages now. It seemed like an awful lot of War Gadgets, but she had no idea how many Albert had.

Suddenly, Albert's hand went up.

"Yes, Albert," said Ms. Haycock.

"May I go to the pencil sharpener, please?"

"Yes, Albert."

Something was up!

Kelly's desk was directly on Albert's way to the pencil sharpener.

Kelly tried to think. She tried to remember what was next on Albert's list of War Gadgets. She went over the list in her mind.

1. Pants Wetter
2. Spitball Cannon
3. ?????????

She couldn't remember. Albert got closer. What was it?

1. Pants Wetter
2. Spitball Cannon
3. ??????????????

48

Kelly felt something tap her lightly on the top of her head just as Albert passed her. Too late she remembered:

3. Smell Gel

An awful smell came from Kelly's hair.

At the pencil sharpener Albert smiled. Then he lifted his finger and gave himself another point in the air. *Gotcha!*

Kelly reached her hand up to the top of her head. She could feel a wad of smelly, gooey gel. She brought her hand down. There was a gooey blob of gel in her hand. It smelled awful. *She* smelled awful.

She quickly stuck her hand into the pocket of her jeans. Her hand in her pocket felt slimy.

She looked at Albert sharpening his pencil. He was still grinning. He would have to walk by Kelly's desk again to get back to his own desk.

When he came by she would be ready. He could not get away with this. She looked at her list of War Gadgets.

What should she use?

Double Gum Shooter?

Lipstick Smear Gun?

Stink Ball?

BRINNNNGGGG! The lunch bell! She would have to get him back later.

She watched Albert hurry back to his desk. He put something shiny and silver into his pocket.

Kelly reached into her backpack and took out the food-fight catapult. She hadn't really planned to use it, but it looked like she might need it after all.

She owed him one now.

He was a creep and he deserved what he would get!

WHOOOOOOSH!!
SQUOOOOOOSH!!

The cafeteria was in the basement of the school. It had tiny windows high up almost to the ceiling. Long tables filled up the floor. At the front of the room was a stoplight.

If the noise in the cafeteria got too loud, Mrs. Hall, the cafeteria attendant, would turn on the yellow light. If the noise got too, too loud, Mrs. Hall would turn on the red light. When the red light went on, all talking had to stop. The kids hated the red light.

The kids lined up to get their lunch trays. Kelly moved through the line.

Good luck: nachos today.

She read the menu on the wall.

NACHOS   GREEN BEANS   ORANGE HALF   MILK

She took her tray and looked for a seat. The only seat she could find was beside Kate Ellen Johnson.

Rats! Kate Ellen would surely say something about her pants or her hair. As she moved toward the table she looked around the cafeteria for Albert. He had to be there somewhere. But where?

She carefully checked all the tables in front of her. Then all the tables to the right of her. Then . . .

Splat!

She felt something hit the side of her head. She looked down on the floor—a green bean.

Oooooooh! The creep strikes again!

She looked around. Yes, there he was across the room. Just wait! The creep was about to pay!

She walked over to Kate Ellen's table.

"Did you have an accident?" Kate Ellen asked in a cutesy voice, looking at Kelly's jeans.

Kelly remembered her wet jeans and turned red.

She didn't answer, she just sat down.

Kate Ellen wrinkled her nose.

"Do you smell something?" she asked.

"*No!*" Kelly said, a little too loud. "I do *not* smell *anything!*"

"Well!" said Kate Ellen, "you don't have to get mad about it!" She turned and began to talk to Sarah in the other seat beside her.

Kelly *was* mad about it! Wet jeans! Smell gel! Spitballs! The creep deserved what he would get!

Kelly looked down at her tray. What would be the best choice for launching? The nachos?

No. The cheese dip would be impressive but the chips were too light.

The orange half? Maybe, it was nice and heavy, and juicy.

The green beans? They had worked pretty well for Albert!

She decided to try the green beans first. She hoped that her aim would be better today.

Everyone was eating and talking. No one noticed Kelly and her food-fight catapult. She picked out a large green bean and loaded it. She pulled back the lever, aimed at Albert, and . . .

Whoooooosh! Squoooooosh!

Direct hit—on the back of Tommy Ballager's head.

Tommy rubbed the back of his head and looked around once. Then he shrugged his shoulders and kept on eating.

Bad aim.

She tried again.

She loaded another green bean and . . .

Whooooosh! Squooooosh!

Direct hit—into Deb Richard's tray. Deb tossed back her hair as if she was insulted. "Disgusting," she said.

Kelly frowned. At this rate she would never get Albert.

She looked down at her tray. Maybe the green beans were too light.

It would have to be the orange. Maybe with a little cheese dip on it. She dipped the orange half into the cheese dip. A little dripped onto the table as she loaded it.

Kate Ellen turned around. She gasped, "Kelly! Whatever are you doing? I mean, you could really get in troub—"

Whooooosh!

The orange flew through the air high above the other kids' heads. It was not headed for Albert. It was headed right for the back of Mrs. Hall's head.

Kelly closed her eyes. She couldn't bear to watch.

Squooooosh!

She heard the orange hit something.

"Did I get Mrs. Hall?" she asked. "I can't look."

"Uh . . . no," Kate Ellen answered. "You definitely didn't get Mrs. Hall."

"Whew! That was close!" said Kelly as she opened her eyes.

She looked up to see where the orange had gone.

At the cafeteria door stood Mr. Hardeman. His face was red. His face was very red. His fists were tight balls. He was looking around the cafeteria, trying to find someone. On top of his head, right in the middle of his bald spot, was an orange half with cheese dip holding it in place.

"You got Hardeman!" Kate Ellen whispered.

Kelly put the food catapult under the table and lowered her eyes.

"I got *Hardeman?*" she said in disbelief.

She didn't look up. She said a prayer that Mr. Hardeman would not see her food-fight catapult.

The red light came on. All the kids got quiet.

"All right, children!" Mr. Hardeman said sternly, "*Who threw that orange?*" He mopped his head with a napkin. A little cheese dip still stuck to his hair.

"I want an answer!" No one spoke.

"Well, let's see now. Someone in here *threw* an orange half, so whoever that person is no longer *has* an orange half. Let's just see who no longer *has* an orange half."

He began to move down the rows of tables, checking the trays. He was on row number one. Three more rows and he would be to Kelly's table.

Kelly put her head down and waited. She was the only kid in the room without any orange and she was only three rows away from Hardeman. There was no gadget in the whole world that could save her now.

She was only three rows away from total doom.

THE MYSTERY PERSON

There was not a sound in the cafeteria as Hardeman moved down the rows of tables. At each table he made the kids hold up their orange halves. Some only had the skins left but they held up whatever they had.

Kelly looked across the room. She saw Albert proudly holding up his orange for Hardeman to see. Hardeman nodded and moved on to the next table.

Everyone was glad that they were not the one kid without an orange half.

Kelly put her head down. She couldn't bear to watch.

Hardeman was getting closer,

closer,

closer . . .

Whooooooooosh! Squoooooooooooosh!!!

Something hit Kelly on the head. She looked down.

A miracle! On the floor beside Kelly's seat was an orange half. She didn't have time to find out who sent it. Quickly, she put the orange half on her tray.

"Now, let's see those oranges!" called out Hardeman at Kelly's table.

Kelly's orange was the first one up. She held it high and thought: *Thank you. Thank you. Thank you, Mystery Person. Whoever you are you have saved me from* TOTAL DOOM.

As soon as Hardeman left she would find her Mystery Person. She would have to find out who saved her.

Hardeman's search was not successful. He turned to leave. Just as he turned, something seemed to catch his eye.

"Young man!" he called out. "You! Over there!"

60

He was pointing at Albert.

"What's that you have in your hand?"

Albert was holding something—something silver. It was the thing that Kelly had seen him slip into his pocket. It was some kind of catapult. He was trying to hold it so that Hardeman couldn't see it. But it was no use.

In what seemed like only three steps Hardeman crossed the room and grabbed the gadget away from Albert.

"Aha!" Hardeman said. "I think we have found our orange shooter."

He looked down at Albert's tray. "No orange half here, either!"

"Young man, I will see *you* in my office in five minutes."

"But . . . but . . ." Albert said.

"But nothing," said Hardeman. "Five minutes!"

He turned sharply and walked out the door.

Still no one made a sound. They all kept looking at Albert.

Slowly he picked up his tray and moved toward the kitchen.

Kelly seemed to be glued in place. One minute ago she had been so terrified for herself and so relieved to get the orange that she hadn't even thought someone else might get in trouble.

Albert was being blamed for something that he hadn't done. Albert was being blamed for something that *she* had done.

She watched Albert walk out the door.

She remembered the pants wetter, the spitball, and the smell gel. A few minutes ago she'd hated Albert so much that she would have done anything to hurt him, but now she felt sorry.

Then she remembered something else. The silver thing that he had was a catapult. *He* had shot the orange! Albert had to be the Mystery Person.

But . . . was he trying to save her or to get back? She would have to think about that later.

Right now there was only one thing to do. One thing that you spend all year in third grade hoping that you will not have to do.

Kelly picked up her tray, took it to the kitchen, and headed for Hardeman's office.

DUM DUM DEE-DUM

A sad tune kept playing over and over in Kelly's mind as she walked down the hall to Hardeman's office.

Dum dum dee-dum, dum dee-dum, dee-dum, dee-dum.

They always played that in her mom's old movies whenever anyone was marching toward their doom. They played it for prisoners headed for execution and for soldiers marching toward a hopeless battle. She even heard them play it once when Bugs Bunny had to march off the end of the high dive at a circus.

It seemed so perfect as she marched toward

Hardeman's office. It was a hopeless situation.

She stood in front of the door. She couldn't make herself go in. She could just slip away . . .

Tap. Tap. Tap.

Quickly she tapped on the door before she could change her mind.

Albert answered the door. He looked surprised to see her. The secretary was at lunch. Albert pointed toward the door of Hardeman's office. It was slightly open.

From inside they could hear the sounds of Hardeman talking to someone on the phone. They didn't dare say a word to each other. They both sat down and waited.

As they waited they could hear the sound of Hardeman's voice talking, but it didn't sound like Hardeman's usual voice. For one thing it sounded higher—and nicer!

Kelly listened. She couldn't figure it out.

She couldn't hear what he was saying but it sounded *nice!*

Hardeman, *nice?* It just couldn't be true.

She heard Hardeman laugh into the phone.

She had never heard him laugh before. It was not a mean kind of snickering laugh but a deep hearty laugh. More like grandpa or a Santa Claus. She couldn't have been more surprised if he had turned a back flip in the hall.

He must be laughing at some evil thing. He was probably laughing at the punishment he would give them. She listened harder.

"Right in the middle of my bald spot!"

Kelly and Albert looked at each other in surprise!

Right in the middle of my bald spot!

He was talking about the orange. He wasn't laughing about their punishment. He was laughing at *himself!*

She had always thought of Hardeman as only a principal. She had never thought of him as a person—especially as a person with a sense of humor.

It was like one of her gadgets. One minute it was one thing, a piece of metal, a piece of bark, tree sap, the next minute you realized that it could be something totally different, too. A paper clip, a cork, an eraser. It all depended on how you looked at it. Or IF you bothered to look at it.

She could always see the potential in things to use for her inventions. When had she stopped seeing the potential in people?

Click!

They heard Hardeman hang up the phone. The time had come.

Hardeman walked out the door toward them.

Dum dum, dee-dum, dum dee-dum, dee-dum, dee-dum.

Now Mr. Hardeman was not smiling. He had his hands clasped behind his back like always. Now his voice was not high and sweet. But somehow thinking of him as a real person made it easier to tell him the truth. Somehow it took away the fear.

"Miss Sparks," he said sternly, "what can I do for *you*?"

"I did it," she answered. The words seemed to rush out too fast.

"What? What *exactly* did you do?"

"The orange, in the cafeteria, I did it, not Albert."

He paused and gave her a hard look.

"I'm surprised, Kelly. That orange could have hurt someone. If it had hit someone in the eye it could have put someone's eye out. Do you understand the danger in what you did?"

Kelly looked at Albert. She had never really thought about hurting him. Not really hurting him, not hitting him in the eye or putting his eye out or anything like that. She had been so busy thinking of him as a creep that she had stopped seeing him as a real person, too.

Her face turned red.

"Kelly, we can't have children throwing food in the cafeteria. I'm going to have to give you a Detention Hall this afternoon. I don't expect to see you in here again."

He turned to Albert. "And you, Albert. Even if you didn't throw that orange, you had a dangerous weapon in the cafeteria. You could have hurt someone, too."

Albert looked down at his feet. "Yes, sir," he answered.

"You can join Kelly in Detention Hall. I'm disappointed to see you in here on your second

day of school. Let's try to keep out of trouble in the future.

"You will both remain in Ms. Haycock's classroom for one half-hour after school. I will personally notify your parents that you will be home late today. You may go now."

I WILL PERSONALLY NOTIFY YOUR PARENTS!!

The words echoed in Kelly's mind as she and Albert walked down the hall back to Ms. Haycock's room.

She thought about Mr. Hardeman calling her mother. Right now he was probably dialing her number.

Now, it was probably ringing.

"Hello?" Her mother was probably answering right now.

"Hello, Mrs. Sparks. Your daughter has been in trouble today."

Kelly's eyes filled with tears. Now the situation was really hopeless! She would be gadget-grounded forever. Albert would be madder than ever at her. He would make even more War Gadgets now!

If only he would stop making War Gadgets, then she could stop, too. After all, he had started the Gadget War in the first place. Shouldn't he be the one to make the first move to stop it?

She remembered the orange. Maybe he already had. But . . . how could she know for sure? Had Albert really tried to save her?

She couldn't imagine a creep like Albert doing something nice like that. Maybe it was time to stop thinking of Albert as only a creep.

Just then she heard Albert sniff. His parents wouldn't be very happy about this, either. Especially in his first week of school. She looked over at Albert walking beside her. Now he didn't seem so tough. In fact, he seemed a lot like her.

As she walked, a plan formed in Kelly's mind. By the time she got back to Ms. Haycock's room she knew what she had to do.

SOMETHING WAS UP!!!

PEACE??

The rest of the afternoon seemed endless.

At 2:30, the final bell rang and the other kids went home. Only Kelly and Albert were left. Kelly looked up at the clock. It would be a long half hour—especially if her plan did not work.

Kelly sat on one side of the room at her desk. Albert sat on the other at his. They did not speak to each other. They did not even look at each other.

Ms. Haycock was not happy about staying after school with them. Soon she left for the teachers' lounge.

Kelly opened her desk and looked at all the gadgets inside. War Gadgets. When she had been making them they seemed so important, so vital. Now they just seemed like pieces of metal and glue.

She picked up the food-fight catapult. She was no longer proud of it.

She stood up. The time had come for Kelly's plan. She hoped it would work.

Albert's head jerked up. He looked worried. He saw the food-fight catapult in her hands and he held his hands up in front of his face as if to protect himself.

This time Kelly was not fighting. This time Kelly had another plan.

He waited to see what she would do.

She gave him a look of determination, then marched up to the front of the room and lifted the top off the trash can.

She looked once more at the food-fight catapult, then smiled at Albert and dropped it in.
Clunk!!
The food-fight catapult clunked into the trash can. Then there was silence.

Albert stared at Kelly for a few seconds.

Kelly held her breath. What would he do?

He stood up.

He opened his desk, took out his Spitball Cannon, and looked at Kelly again.

Then he headed for the trash can.

Clunk!!

In went the cannon.

It was his turn to smile.

Kelly's breath came out in one long *whoosh*.

The next few minutes were crazy.

Kelly ran back to her desk for her next War Gadget.

Clunk!! In went the Spy Snooper.

Then Albert.

Clunk!! In went the jar of Smell Gel.

Clunk! went the Fake Pencil.

Clunk! went the Sticky Chalk.

Clunk! Clunk! Clunk! went all the War Gadgets one by one until the last one was in the trash can.

Kelly and Albert stood on either side of the trash can, out of breath, looking down at the War Gadgets.

Then Albert reached out his hand to Kelly. Kelly looked up in surprise. Was it another trick? A buzzer? A shocker?

Only one way to find out. She put out her hand.

They shook hands over the pile of gadgets.

"Peace?" Albert said.

"Peace!" Kelly answered.

It felt good.

Making peace was definitely nicer than making war.

Whatever problems she would have later on at home now seemed small. This one time she had solved her problem by herself—without her gadgets. Maybe it was time to stop thinking of herself as only a Gadget Wiz!

Kelly smiled at Albert.

"Albert Einstein Jones," she said, "I think you have potential after all!"

"Kelly Sparks," he answered, "I think you have some potential yourself!"

They took one last look at the pile of War Gadgets, then together they closed the trash can.

THE GADGET WAR WAS OVER!